S0-AAE-018

GHOST ✦ DETECTORS

The Spelling Bee Specter!

BOOK 19

BY
ADRIENNE ENDERLE

ILLUSTRATED BY
DAVE SHEPHARD

Calico

An Imprint of Magic Wagon
abdopublishing.com

To Dotti, thank you for all your guidance, wisdom, and encouragement —AE
A special thanks to my Melissa —DS

abdopublishing.com

Published by Magic Wagon, a division of ABDO, PO Box 398166, Minneapolis, Minnesota 55439. Copyright © 2016 by Abdo Consulting Group, Inc. International copyrights reserved in all countries. No part of this book may be reproduced in any form without written permission from the publisher. Calico™ is a trademark and logo of Magic Wagon.

Printed in the United States of America, North Mankato, Minnesota.
042015
092015

 **THIS BOOK CONTAINS RECYCLED MATERIALS**

Written by Adrienne Enderle
Illustrated by Dave Shephard
Edited by Rochelle Baltzer, Heidi M.D. Elston,
        Megan M. Gunderson & Bridget O'Brien
Designed by Jillian O'Brien

Library of Congress Cataloging-in-Publication Data

Enderle, Adrienne, author.
  The spelling bee specter! / by Adrienne Enderle ; illustrated by David Shephard.
     pages cm. -- (Ghost detectors ; Book 19)
  Summary: Dandy is already worried about the fifth grade spelling bee, because his family has a history of winning--and once it starts, things keep going wrong, and his best friend Malcolm realizes that the contest is being haunted and the boys need to find out why and banish the specter.
  ISBN 978-1-62402-102-2 (alk. paper)
1. Ghost stories. 2. Spelling bees--Juvenile fiction. 3. Contests--Juvenile fiction. 4. Best friends--Juvenile fiction. [1. Ghosts--Fiction. 2. Spelling bees--Fiction. 3. Contests--Fiction. 4. Best friends--Fiction. 5. Friendship--Fiction. 6. Humorous stories.] I. Shephard, David (Illustrator), illustrator. II. Title.

  PZ7.1.E52Sp 2016
  813.6--dc23
  [Fic]

                    2015003012

Contents

Chapter 1
A Family Tradition

Malcolm's eyes crossed as he looked down at the next word on the spelling list. They all ran together like a big, blurry sentence. "Terrific," he said.

"Terrific," Dandy repeated, scrunching his face to think. "T-e-r-r-i-f-i-c. Terrific."

"Terrific," Malcolm repeated.

Dandy gave Malcolm a confused look. "I just spelled *terrific*."

"I know," Malcolm said. "And you did a terrific job."

Dandy groaned. "Not funny."

"Can we take a break now?" Malcolm asked as he turned on his specter detector so his ghost dog, Spooky, could come out to play. Spooky instantly appeared and jumped at the word list in Malcolm's hand.

Yip! Yip!

Dandy sat back and draped his arm over his eyes. "We can't take a break. Not yet. The spelling bee is tomorrow."

Malcolm sighed. "All right. A few more." He looked down at the next word on the page. "Unusual."

"Unusual." Dandy twitched his mouth. He looked up at Malcolm. "May I have the definition please?"

Malcolm ran his finger across the page as he read. "Strange, odd, or weird." He smiled. "Like spending Friday night

studying for a spelling bee, when we could be doing something fun."

Dandy frowned. "Never mind," he said, snatching the word list from Malcolm's hand.

They'd been at this for so long Malcolm was starting to get a headache. And not just any headache. This was the same kind he got when he had to listen to his older sister, Cocoa, practice her choir solo. She had the voice of a screeching violin. But Dandy was his best friend, and he couldn't let him down.

"No, it's okay," he told Dandy. "I want to help. But can we grab a snack or something? I mean, seriously, it's just a spelling bee."

Dandy gulped as his eyes bulged. "*Just* a spelling bee? Malcolm, this is more than *just* a spelling bee. It's a family tradition."

He paused and mumbled, "Tradition. T-r-a-d-i-t-i-o-n. Tradition."

"I get it," Malcolm said, teasing Spooky with a plastic dog bone. "Your family is made up of good spellers."

"Have you seen our trophy case?" Dandy asked. "When my dad was a kid, he won the spelling bee three years straight. His father won it four times. And his father's father was so good they had to invent new words just to keep the contest going. There's no way I'm going to let my family down, Malcolm."

Malcolm doubted Dandy's great-grandfather caused the invention of new words. But there was no point arguing with his best friend.

"Okay. I wouldn't want to ruin your family's t-r-a-d-i-t-i-o-n, Dandy." Malcolm

straightened the spelling list and read the next word out loud. "Peace."

Dandy took a deep breath. "Peace. Can I hear it in a sentence, please?"

Malcolm shrugged. "Sure. Every beauty queen wants world peace."

"Peace. P-e-a-c-e."

Malcolm shot Dandy a thumbs-up. "Terrific. Next word. Despair."

"Despair." Dandy's eyes squinted in thought. "D-e-s . . . p-a . . . r-e."

Malcolm did a thumbs-down. "Despair. D-e-s-p-a-i-r."

Dandy collapsed back dramatically, spooking Spooky. The phantom dog skittered away and hid inside the wall.

"I'm doomed!" Dandy cried. "It's hopeless! No one will ever invent words because of me."

"Don't be so sure," Malcolm said, thinking of a couple right away. He stood up and stretched.

"Besides, even if I make it to the second round," Dandy said, "who knows what eerie stuff might happen."

Malcolm raised an eyebrow. "It's at the community center, Dandy, not a spooky old mansion."

Dandy sat up, looking at Malcolm. "But I heard the community center is haunted."

"No way," said Malcolm. "Nothing in this town is haunted without me knowing about it."

After all, Malcolm and Dandy called themselves the Ghost Detectors. They had been tracking ghosts ever since Malcolm bought his Ecto-Handheld-Automatic-Heat-Sensitive-Laser-Enhanced Specter Detector. The ghost finder worked like a charm!

Still, Malcolm powered up his computer, just to check. He typed in the words *haunted community center* and narrowed his search to their area.

"Whoa!" Malcolm exclaimed, scanning through all the hits. "It says here that twenty years ago during the sixth grade spelling bee, when a guy was asked to spell *opera*, he sang instead."

Dandy looked like he might throw up. "Please don't let that happen to me."

Malcolm continued reading the article. "The boy insisted that something made him do it." He scrolled down. "And look at this. Twelve years ago during the fourth grade spelling bee, a girl made it all the way to state finals, and then she started using sign language instead of speaking."

"I don't have to worry about that," Dandy said. "I don't know sign language."

Malcolm tilted his head. "According to this, neither did she."

Dandy gulped.

"Oh man," Malcolm said, shaking his head.

Dandy leaned in. "What?"

"Four years ago during the fifth grade spelling bee, every time a boy tried to spell *mischief*, his pants would drop."

Sweat beads popped out on Dandy's forehead. "Oh no. Maybe I should wear suspenders."

Malcolm sat back, scratching his chin. "This is bad."

"I know," Dandy said. "I told you the community center was haunted."

Malcolm turned and looked him in the eye. "No, Dandy, the community center isn't haunted . . . the spelling bee is!"

Dandy sat up and hugged his knees. "I think I need some ice cream. Two scoops."

Chapter 2
Super Savers

Malcolm bounded into the kitchen, excited to dig in to some delicious ice cream. His feet slid across the floor as his socks lost their grip on the tile.

Malcolm's arms flailed in large circles and he lost his balance, falling sideways. His left hip knocked against the kitchen table, scattering everything lying on top.

"Careful!" Malcolm's mom hurried to the table. But instead of checking to see if he was okay, she worried over the tiny bits

of paper that had fallen to the floor. She picked up a few and sighed. "Now everything is out of order." She had an irked expression on her face. It was the same look Cocoa had after their dad told her she couldn't dye her hair neon green.

"What are those?" Malcolm asked as he rubbed the new bruise forming on his leg.

Grandma Eunice rolled into the room. She squealed her wheelchair to a stop. "They're coupons. Your mom and I joined Super Savers."

Super Savers? It sounded like a league of superheroes. Malcolm cut his eyes from his great-grandma to his mom, then back. Impossible. "What's Super Savers? Are you going to wear a cape and a mask?"

"It's a coupon club," Grandma Eunice answered. "We clip coupons from the

Avon Public Library

newspaper and earn points. I've already saved a ton on denture cream, toilet paper, and floor polish."

Malcolm glanced down at his socks. That explained the slippery floor.

Grandma Eunice smiled wide, blue denture cream oozing across her gums. "Whoever saves the most money at the end of the week wins a BIG PRIZE!"

Malcolm's mom smiled. "It's not *that* big," she said, putting the coupons back in order. "It's just a twenty dollar gift card to ShopMart."

That sounded pretty big to Malcolm. He thought of all the stuff twenty dollars could buy, like a video game or a movie or endless snacks. He could even buy some headphones that would block out Cocoa's grumbling.

Grandma Eunice picked a coupon from the table and waved it under her nose. "I smell victory!" She flashed another denture cream smile. "And you know the best part? I'm going to beat Trudy Pembersmock."

"Don't start celebrating yet," Malcolm's mom said.

Grandma Eunice waggled a finger. "Just you wait. That old ninny wins everything, but she won't win that twenty dollars!"

"You're just upset that she won the grand prize at bingo last week," Malcolm's mom explained.

"You're darn tootin'! And it won't happen again. I'll see to it." Grandma Eunice popped a wheelie and whizzed out of the room.

Malcolm limped to the fridge, careful not to slip again. He had no idea who

Trudy Pembersmock was, but boy, he sure wouldn't want to be her. She wouldn't want Grandma Eunice on her bad side! Opening the freezer, Malcolm grabbed the ice cream container and pried open the lid.

Huh?

He frowned at his mom. "Where's the chocolate?"

"We ran out," she said. "But we had a coupon for blueberry. Saved fifty cents."

Malcolm looked down at it. It was the color of Grandma Eunice's blue denture cream. Then he noticed green spots. "Why are there bits of green?"

"That's kale," his mom told him. "We got it at the health food store."

"Eew!" Malcolm's stomach flip-flopped. He popped the lid back on and put the container in the freezer. He didn't know

exactly what kale was, but to him, pretty much anything green was gross.

Malcolm left the kitchen and hobbled back to the basement. Dandy sat with his back to the door, an enormous dictionary plopped open on his lap. It was so huge Malcolm couldn't see Dandy's crisscrossed legs underneath it.

"Do you know what kale is?" Malcolm asked.

Dandy's face twisted in terror. "No. Why? Is it on the list?" He frantically turned to it in the dictionary. "Kale," Dandy said. "Noun. A type of cabbage with crinkled leaves. K-a-l-e. Kale."

Ugh! Cabbage in ice cream? Malcolm sure hoped Grandma Eunice won that gift card. Then maybe he could talk her into buying some real ice cream.

Chapter 3
Let the Spelling Bee-gin!

Malcolm biked to Dandy's house the next morning. It was so early there was dew on the neighbors' lawns.

His stomach rumbled as he leaned his bicycle on its kickstand. He'd left without eating. After last night's dinner of cow tongue, potato skins, and something that looked like boogers, Malcolm felt it was safer to eat breakfast at the Dees' house.

He knocked on the front door three times before it opened.

"You're not dressed yet," Malcolm said, looking at Dandy's Iron Man pajamas.

Dandy yawned loudly, rubbing sleep gunk from his eyes. "I was up all night studying," he replied. "I need to know the words on the list backward and forward."

Malcolm rolled his eyes. "Dandy, they aren't going to make you spell them backward."

Dandy shook his head, eyes wide. "You never know. When my great-grandpa Wilber was in the spelling bee, the judges made up new words for him to spell."

"No way."

"Yes way," Dandy said. "That's where the word *elbow* came from."

"I'm sure the word *elbow* is older than your great-grandfather." Then Malcolm remembered Grandma Eunice was his

great-grandma. That woman had probably invented the wheel. "Or maybe not."

Right then his stomach growled louder than a revving car engine. "Got anything to eat that doesn't have kale in it?"

Dandy changed out of his pj's and into a dressy blue shirt, black pants with stiff creases, and black shoes that shone brighter than a nickel on the sidewalk in summer.

"Dude," Malcolm said, approving of his friend's new gussied-up look.

Dandy beamed. "I know."

They entered the kitchen to find bacon, eggs, and buttered toast waiting for them.

Malcolm envied Dandy. Not only was he an only child, but he didn't have to eat gross green food.

"Good morning, boys!" Mrs. Dee said as Malcolm and Dandy sat down at the table. "Be sure to eat everything on your plate. An empty stomach is no one's friend."

Dandy chewed his lip, looking worried. "I'm too nervous. What goes down might come back up."

Hopefully not onstage! Malcolm thought.

"Don't worry, honey," Mrs. Dee said. She walked around the table and pulled Dandy into a bone-crushing hug. "You'll be amazing, I just know it. I've already made room in the trophy cabinet," she said, pointing at the display.

"Mooooom," Dandy whined.

"Leave the poor kid alone, Diana," Mr. Dee said, walking into the kitchen. "You're suffocating him."

Mrs. Dee let Dandy go.

"Suffocate," Dandy repeated. "S-u-f-f-o-c-a-t-e. Suffocate."

Mr. Dee beamed. "That's my boy!"

Malcolm rode with Dandy's family to the community center, where a large banner hung above the front doors.

WELCOME TO THE 5TH GRADE SPELLING BEE

Even though they'd arrived early, the place was bustling with people. The contestants gathered. Everyone was all dressed up. Parents hovered, grinning and snapping pictures.

The registration table was way in the back. Malcolm followed Dandy as they threaded their way through the mob. The

contestants sounded like a spelling choir rehearsing a dozen different songs at once.

"Name?" a woman sitting at the table asked from behind a sky-high stack of papers. They couldn't see her mouth, but her eyes narrowed at them.

"Daniel Dee," Dandy answered.

There was shuffling behind the paper tower. Then the woman looked at Dandy again. "Was that *Dee*? Spell it, please."

Dandy stood still, staring. His mouth opened and closed, but no words uttered forth.

Oh great, Malcolm thought. *If he can't remember how to spell his name, how's he going to remember how to spell* elbow*?*

"D-e-e," Malcolm answered.

After some more shuffling, an arm reached over the paper pile and handed

Dandy a large, yellow envelope. "Your number is inside, Mr. Dee," she said, "and your name will be taped to the back of your seat."

Dandy stayed frozen, looking down at the envelope. Malcolm nudged him.

"Thanks," Dandy squeaked. Then he quickly turned around and scurried off, his shiny shoes clip-clopping on the hard floor.

Malcolm rushed to catch up.

The contestants and guests trickled into the auditorium. One by one, the kids mounted the stage and took their seats. Malcolm gave Dandy a thumbs-up as Dandy slowly inched onto his chair.

Squeeeeeak!

All eyes turned to Dandy. He shifted a little and . . .

Squeeeeeak!

This was not just any old squeak. It was like nails on a chalkboard, echoing off the walls and raising goose bumps on Malcolm's arms.

Dandy leaned down to scratch his ankle.

Squeeeeeak!

Malcolm gave Dandy the OK symbol, hoping that would put him at ease.

A pudgy man wearing a gray suit and loafers stepped up to the microphone. His black hair was slicked back, plastered to his head. Malcolm wasn't sure what kind of hair gel the guy used, but it resembled the oil patches he'd seen puddled under old cars.

"Welcome to this year's annual fifth grade spelling bee competition," the man boomed. "I am your spelling bee master, Ronald McDonaldson."

The crowd snickered.

The man's face reddened as his eyebrows dipped. "McDonald*son*. I don't sell hamburgers."

Malcolm wished he did. The last time he looked in the freezer, he saw a jumbo box of veggie patties. *Blech!* Bought with a Super Savers coupon, of course.

"So now," Mr. McDonaldson said, "let the spelling bee-gin!" He stepped back and took a deep bow. As he was bending . . .

Squeeeeeak!

The audience roared with laughter.

The bee master shot straight up, his face the color of a tomato. He spun around and glared at Dandy.

Dandy shrugged and mouthed, "Oops."

Chapter 4

The First Contestants

Mr. McDonaldson sat with his back to the audience. The auditorium lights reflected off his slimy hair. Malcolm blinked against the glare. It was like staring at the sun.

Mr. McDonaldson spoke into his microphone. "Contestant number one."

The tallest fifth-grader Malcolm had ever seen loped up to center stage. Malcolm double-checked to see if he was wearing stilts. Nope. The kid was all legs!

"Ahem." Mr. McDonaldson cleared his throat. "Your word is *tremble*."

Contestant number one smiled wide, revealing silver braces almost as shiny as Mr. McDonaldson's hair. "Tremble," he repeated. "T-r-e-m-b-l-e. Tremble."

"That is correct."

The audience clapped wildly.

The kid jutted his chin, nodding. "That was an easy one." He turned and strutted back to his seat on his lanky legs.

Mr. McDonaldson cleared his throat again. "Ahem. Contestant number two."

A girl hopped to her feet and shuffled up. Her blonde hair was tied in a braid so long Rapunzel would've been jealous. She gulped, waiting for her word.

Mr. McDonaldson leaned into his mic. "Your word is *suspense*."

"Sssussspense," she said, her voice shaking while mists of spit spattered out.

Yikes! Malcolm thought. She was so nervous she was a walking squirt gun. Malcolm was out of spitting range, but he cringed every time the letter *s* came up. And there were a lot of them.

The girl continued. "ESSS-U-ESSS . . ." She sprayed so much moisture Malcolm wondered if a rainbow might appear. " . . . p-e-n . . ." Malcolm squinted, waiting for the next shot of spittle on the final *s*. " . . . c-e," she finished with pride. "Sssussspense."

Buzzzzzzz.

"I'm sorry," Mr. McDonaldson said. "That's incorrect."

"That'sss impossssssssible!" the girl cried, giving the floor another spit shine.

Mr. McDonaldson shook his head. "The correct spelling is s-u-s-p-e-n-s-e."

The girl burst into tears. "That'ssss not fair! I should get a ssssecond chance! Thissss contessst isss rigged!"

If she doesn't stop whining, they'll have to bring out the mop, Malcolm thought.

Mr. McDonaldson slicked back his already slicked-back hair. "I'm sorry. Better luck next year."

The girl frowned, twisting her massive braid in her hands as she stomped off the stage. There was now an empty spot onstage, waiting to be filled. Finally Mr. McDonaldson said, "Contestant number three, you're up."

Contestant number three? That was . . .

Dandy froze in his chair. His eyes went wide with fear.

"Contestant number three," Mr. McDonaldson repeated.

Dandy bit his lip and slowly slipped out of his chair. *Squeeeeeak!*

Chapter 5
Buzzzz!

Dandy shuffled up to the microphone, his shiny shoes gleaming in the spotlight. His fists were balled at his sides. Malcolm could plainly see his best friend was suffering from stage fright.

"Ahem!" Mr. McDonaldson loudly cleared his throat, like there was an actual frog stuck inside. "Your word is *guitar.*"

Tricky, Malcolm thought. He hoped Dandy would remember the silent *u.*

"G-u-i-t-a—" Dandy's voice quivered.

BUZZZZZZZ.

It was so loud Malcolm clapped his hands over his ears. Almost everyone else did, too.

Mr. McDonaldson adjusted the button. "I'm sorry. There seems to be—"

BUZZZZZZZZZZZZZZZZZZZZZZZZZZZZZ.

The grating noise caused goose bumps to prickle Malcolm's arms. Dandy hunkered down, like he was ducking a fly ball.

Mr. McDonaldson snatched up the big red button and banged it against the table a couple times. Silence fell.

"Finally," he said, slicking back his hair again. "I'm so sorry, contestant number three. You may continue."

Dandy slowly rose, prying his hands from his ears. "Were you speaking to me?"

Poor Dandy, Malcolm thought. *Standing*

that close to the buzzer, his ears must be ringing.

Mr. McDonaldson jutted his chin. "You may begin again."

Dandy nodded. "Guitar. G-u-i-t-a—"

BUZZZZZZZZZZZZZZZZZZZZZZZZZZZ.

Mr. McDonaldson slammed his fists down on the table. "Could someone please get rid of this stupid thing?"

A woman scurried down the center aisle.

She looked like the same lady who had checked in Dandy behind the stacks of paper.

She grabbed the buzzer with both hands and stretched out her arms like she was holding a ticking time bomb. She power walked back through the audience. The noise grew louder as she hurried, like it had a mind of its own. The auditorium doors slammed behind her, bringing some peace and quiet to the room.

Mr. McDonaldson let out a long breath. "At last." He smoothed his suit. "Try again, son."

Dandy jiggled his finger in his ear and stood taller. "Guitar. G-u-i-t-a—"

Then the microphone went dead.

Chapter 6
A Sneaking Suspicion

It looked like Dandy had formed the last letter. His mouth moved, opening and closing like a hungry goldfish. But no one heard his voice.

Then Mr. McDonaldson started yelling. "Oh, for goodness' sake! Would someone turn the kid's mic back on?"

The woman reappeared, huffing as she scurried to the stage. She fiddled with the microphone switch. "Testing." Her voice boomed through the crowd. "Testing.

Testing one, two, three. Testing one, two, three, four."

"Okay! Okay! It's working!" Mr. McDonaldson bellowed. A piece of his hair had become unslicked. It poked out over his ear like a pointing finger.

The woman smiled and gestured for Dandy to continue.

"Once again," Mr. McDonaldson said, "your word is *guitar*."

Dandy stood tall. "Guitar. G-u-i-t-a—" He suddenly went fish-mouthed. The mic had died again.

"Unbelievable!" Mr. McDonaldson cried. He swiveled around to face the audio booth at the back of the auditorium. His face was as purple as a turnip and his poking piece of hair jiggled when he barked, "What in the green grapes is going on up there?"

Everyone shifted, looking back. One of the audio guys shrugged.

"Fix it!" Mr. McDonaldson yelled.

Malcolm had a sneaking suspicion. His eyes followed the microphone cord, which snaked all the way backstage. *Hmm.*

The audience, in a whispering frenzy, paid no attention as Malcolm snuck behind the curtain. He walked along by the cord until he came to the power outlet. Just as he'd suspected. It was unplugged.

Malcolm pushed the power cord back in tight. A loud screech of feedback followed. A moment later he heard the huffy lady say, "Testing one, two, three."

Malcolm hurried back to the side of the stage to watch Dandy spell.

"Ahem," Dandy said. Then he continued. "G-u—"

Silence.

Malcolm quickly turned. The plug was once again lying on the ground. There was no one around but him. He went back over and plugged it in. To be sure it was in tight, he wiggled it a little.

"Testing," he heard from the stage.

Malcolm waited by the power outlet. A moment later, Dandy's voice rang out loud and clear. "G-u—" Then nothing.

Malcolm looked down. The cord was unplugged again. A chill traveled down Malcolm's spine. He looked right and left. Even though there was no one around, he knew he had company.

"Ohhh no you don't," he said, pushing the plug back into the wall.

It popped right back out.

He shoved it in again.

Pop! It landed on the floor.

This time, when Malcolm picked it up, something tried to snatch it from his hands.

"Hey," he said, pulling the cord. Something pulled back.

Malcolm tugged.

It tugged.

It looked like a one-person tug-of-war.

"Let go!" Malcolm demanded. It did.

Humph! Malcolm tumbled back, knocking into a shelf. "Ow!" He hurried to plug the mic back in, blocking it with his body so nothing could pull it away.

Once again, Dandy started up. "G-u-i—"

BUZZZZZZZZZZZZZZZZZZZZZZZZZZZZ.

Impossible, Malcolm thought. *Did they bring the buzzer back?*

Right then, someone hollered, "BEES!"

Chapter 7
An Outrage!

Screams erupted from the audience. Malcolm peeked into the auditorium.

Thousands of bees had swarmed in, buzzing and whirling like a tornado. People scattered, flailing their arms, swatting the air, and stumbling over each other.

Mr. McDonaldson cowered under his table. "Shoo! Shoo!"

Malcolm didn't see Dandy. He had probably scrambled through the back door to look for his parents in the parking lot.

A hefty swarm of bees hummed after Malcolm. Malcolm hurried to the backstage exit and charged out into the glaring sunlight. The crowd was still screaming like Godzilla had attacked. Malcolm ran to the Dees' car and waited.

Then, he saw Mr. Dee, Mrs. Dee, and . . . a giant, walking shirt? Malcolm realized Dandy had pulled his shirt over his head to block the bees. He stumbled along next to his parents, bumping into cars.

"Ridiculous!" Mrs. Dee barked as she unlocked the car. "How could the city not know there were colonies of bees nesting on public property? It's an outrage!"

"Outrage," Dandy mumbled from beneath his shirt. "O-u-t-r-a-g-e."

Malcolm grabbed the neck of Dandy's shirt and popped it back down in place. Then in his

lowest voice he whispered, "What happened in there wasn't just a series of weird events."

"Really?" Dandy whispered back. "'Cause it seemed pretty weird to me."

"But it gets even weirder."

Dandy's eyebrows perked, waiting.

"You were right." Malcolm leaned right next to Dandy's ear. "This spelling bee is haunted."

"Hurry," Malcolm said to Dandy, waiting in Dandy's bedroom while he changed clothes. "We still have to go to my house to pick up the specter detector and the ghost zapper so we can hunt down this spelling bee specter."

"Okay, I'm ready." Dandy came trudging out of his closet decked out in full hockey

gear. In front of his helmet he'd attached a kitchen strainer. He held his giant dictionary in one hand and a can of wasp spray in the other.

Malcolm blinked. "You're seriously going to wear that?"

Dandy nodded, the strainer bobbing. "Those bees meant business."

"Yeah, well, so do we," Malcolm said. "But why the dictionary?"

Dandy dropped it to the ground. *Wham!* "I figure I can squash at least ten bees at a time with it."

Ten toes at a time, too, Malcolm thought. He nodded toward the door. "Let's go."

The boys rushed to Malcolm's house. They dashed inside and Malcolm—*bam!*—slammed headfirst into a huge metal contraption that looked like a snaky jungle

gym. He rubbed his head, wishing he'd been wearing a helmet too.

Dandy lifted his strainer and gawked. "Uh . . . Malcolm, there's a spaceship in your living room."

It did have a UFO look to it.

"What is this?" Malcolm said, feeling the goose egg forming on his noggin.

From somewhere in the middle of the metal maze, Grandma Eunice said, "It's my new Crazy-Fit-Fat-Fighting Exercise Machine."

Malcolm looked through the bars at his great-grandma perched in her wheelchair. How she had gotten in there he'd never know! She wore a pink flowered shirt and egg yolk yellow yoga pants.

"An exercise machine?" Malcolm asked.

"Yep," she replied. "Your old granny is going to get buff and beautiful."

Ew, Malcolm thought.

"And even better," Grandma Eunice went on, "I got thirty percent off with Super Savers."

That explained it.

"Watch this!" she said.

Malcolm was still seeing double from whacking his head, but he watched anyway. Dandy's eyes were glued to her too.

She spit on each of her palms, rubbed them together, and grabbed a triangle object dangling over her head. She pulled herself up . . . up . . . up . . . about an inch off her chair. Her face turned redder than a crayon and she made a bunch of rude grunting noises. "Look at me!" she uttered through a series of groans.

"Yeah," Malcolm said. "That's . . . great."

Dandy let the strainer drop back down over his face. Malcolm figured he'd seen enough.

Grandma Eunice let go of the triangle and landed—*plop!*—back in her chair. She

grinned, flashing her denture cream. "And check this out," she wheezed.

Malcolm held up his hand. "I don't know, Grandma. Maybe you shouldn't overdo it."

"Overdo it?" she gasped. "I'm only getting started."

That's what scared Malcolm the most.

Grandma Eunice spun her chair around, hooked her feet in something that looked like an electronic boogie board, and pressed a button. The board went zooming up and down and tilted side to side, bringing her with it. Grandma Eunice twisted and turned, holding her arms out like a surfer catching a killer wave. "Wheeeeee!"

Malcolm had to admit, it did look like fun. More fun than exercise.

It finally came to a stop, tilting and dropping Grandma Eunice back in her chair.

"Did you see that?" she hooted, looking proud. "I just worked off ten calories."

"Yeah, that's great," Malcolm told her.

Dandy nodded in agreement, the strainer tapping against his neck.

Grandma Eunice clacked her dentures. "Trudy doesn't stand a chance. I'm going to win the Super Savers prize *and* look better than her."

"But," Malcolm said, eyeing the huge contraption, "is it going to stay in the living room? It's blocking the TV."

She turned in a circle. "Hmm . . . maybe we can . . . hmm . . ."

Malcolm sighed. He nudged Dandy. "Come on. We need to get going."

"It's a nice exerciser," Dandy said as he and Malcolm climbed over chains and bars to get across the room.

Grandma Eunice winked. "Thanks, Dandydoo."

When they got to the basement, Dandy said, "She's really strong. Did you see her veins popping out?"

"They're always popping out," Malcolm said.

"But are they always that purple?"

Malcolm thought about it. "Yeah."

He flipped on his specter detector to make sure it was fully powered.

Yip! Yip! Spooky appeared, ready to play.

"No time," Malcolm said to the pooch. "We'll play phantom catch later. Promise."

Spooky curled up in the corner while Malcolm packed the gear.

"Do we have everything?" Dandy asked.

Malcolm flung his pack over his shoulder and nodded. "Let's do this."

Chapter 8
Books Can Open Doors

Malcolm's mind whirled as he and Dandy pedaled their bikes to the community center. They knew little about this ghost. Had it attacked other events or did it just hate spelling bees? Either way, they'd send this specter p-a-c-k-i-n-g.

"How will we get in?" Dandy asked, huffing as they rode uphill. Sweat dribbled down his pasta strainer face guard.

"Hopefully we'll just walk in the front door," Malcolm answered. But as

they wheeled into the parking lot, the idea vanished like a magician's coin. Mr. McDonaldson stood at the entrance, gesturing wildly to a man in a gray uniform. The man had his foot on the bumper of a truck that read:

"What do you mean there are no bees?" Mr. McDonaldson boomed, his hair sticking out all over, now fluffy and wild.

Dandy raised the strainer, his eyes flat. "Wow, if Mr. McD had plastic goggles he'd look like a mad scientist."

"No kidding," Malcolm said. "Come on, don't let him see us."

"Listen," the other man said as the boys rode past, "I found no signs of a beehive anywhere. Not in the rafters, the eaves, the plumbing, or the electrical closets. Unless you want me to start tearing out walls."

Mr. McDonaldson looked like he was ready to start tearing out his hair. "No!"

The man in the uniform shrugged. "Fine. Where should I send the bill?"

"Gah!" Mr. McDonaldson bellowed.

Malcolm and Dandy circled to the back.

"So much for walking right in," Malcolm said as he chained his bicycle to a rack near a loading ramp.

Dandy pulled his colossal dictionary and wasp spray from the basket of his bike. "What are we going to do now?"

Malcolm nodded to a rolling door by the ramp. It was raised just enough to slip

under. Even Dandy's bulky hockey suit should fit. "Come on."

Malcolm went first, dropping flat. He belly crawled, scooching with his elbows till he was on the other side. The area was dark and smelled like fresh-cut lumber. He stood for a moment, then said, "Dandy, what are you waiting for?"

Finally, Dandy's helmet came sliding through. Then the strainer. Next, Dandy's head poked through. He waggled like a toppled windup toy. But before he made it all the way in, the chains began to crank. The rolling door inched down.

"Hurry, Dandy!" Malcolm urged.

Dandy squirmed like a wriggly eel.

The door continued to close.

Malcolm reached for Dandy's hand to pull him in, but Dandy's hands were full.

"Hurry!" he repeated, worried that Dandy was about to be crushed.

But instead of crawling for his life, Dandy's face lit up. He quickly pushed the dictionary in place. The door came to a creaking stop when it hit the giant book. Dandy, with little room to spare, pulled himself inside.

Malcolm sighed with relief.

Dandy picked up his helmet and strainer and gazed down at his dictionary wedged under the door. "You know how Mrs. Goolsby is always telling us that books can open doors?"

"Yeah," Malcolm said, thinking of their fifth grade teacher's favorite phrase. "But I don't think this is what she meant."

Chapter 9
A Spelling Quiz

Dandy knelt and tugged at his dictionary. "I can't leave the dictionary here."

"Sure you can," Malcolm said, his hands wavering. "This might be our only way out."

Panic crossed Dandy's face.

"It's not like we'll need to look up any words," Malcolm assured him.

"But this dictionary is my good luck charm. It's the one my dad used to help him win the spelling bee three years in a row. And I need all the luck I can get!"

"Dandy, there's nothing lucky about getting trapped in here."

Dandy's mouth twitched. He stroked his chin. He snapped his fingers and grinned. "Got it." In one swift move, he kicked out the dictionary and shoved his helmet in its place, just as the door was about to crank down another fraction.

Malcolm nodded. "Good thinking." He powered up the specter detector. "It's time to save the spelling bee."

Malcolm pointed the way as they slinked through a long, dark hallway to an area backstage. He flipped on a light switch, casting a glow on a stack of chairs and a whiteboard listing upcoming events. He checked the power outlet. The mic was plugged in.

"Where are you?" Malcolm mumbled, turning in a circle.

The specter detector suddenly kicked in. *Bleep-bleep-bleep.*

The boys froze.

"It's here somewhere," Malcolm said. He slowly swept the detector left and right, searching for the ghost.

That's when another sound filled the area. *Cheepa-cheepa-cheepa.* The noise raised the hairs on Malcolm's arms and made him shiver.

Dandy pointed to the whiteboard. "Uh, Malcolm."

The schedule that was written on the board disappeared in wide circles, like someone was erasing it. Once the board had been wiped clean, an invisible marker squeaked out:

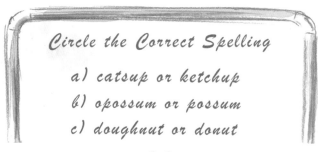

Circle the Correct Spelling

a) catsup or ketchup

b) opossum or possum

c) doughnut or donut

Malcolm sighed, rolling his eyes. "Really? You're trying to trick us with a spelling quiz?"

Dandy nudged Malcolm. "Don't worry," he whispered. "I've got this." He set down his dictionary and sauntered over to the whiteboard, head held high. He popped his neck, cracked his knuckles, and picked up a blue marker.

Malcolm gulped, thinking about earlier when Dandy couldn't remember how to spell his last name. "Uh . . . you sure about this?"

"P-o-s-i-t-i-v-e," Dandy spelled as he uncapped the marker.

Malcolm cringed, waiting.

Instead of circling an answer, Dandy wrote the words *All of the above*.

Suddenly Dandy's dictionary flew up into the air and—*thunk!*—whacked him on the head.

"Wrong! Wrong! Wrong!" a deep voice boomed out from all around them.

"Ouch!" Dandy threw his arms over his head as the dictionary walloped him in the head again.

Malcolm had no idea where the voice had come from. It pushed into his ears from everywhere. He swiveled around, trying to find the ghost. But there was nothing except Dandy . . . and his floating dictionary.

"Stop it!" Dandy yelled, as he ran around the room. But the dictionary chased after him, whacking him again. And again. *Thunk! Thunk! Thunk!*

"Hold on," Malcolm said. He unzipped his backpack and dug out his ghost zapper. "I'll get him."

Dandy darted around, flinging his arms as he tried to bat away the flying dictionary.

"Why are you doing this? I got it right," he wailed.

"No, you didn't!" the voice said.

Malcolm swiveled toward the door. There at the entrance stood the glowing figure of a man.

Chapter 10
Bernie Baxter

The ghost's white hair bristled and his bushy eyebrows waggled as he stared daggers at Malcolm.

That wimpy guy is causing this? Malcolm thought. He pointed the zapper at the ghost. "Stop whomping my friend, or I'll zap you into a purple puddle."

The ghost raised one of his caterpillar eyebrows. "Oh?" *Flash!* He disappeared. The dictionary dropped to the floor and the specter detector stopped beeping.

Malcolm kept the zapper up as he turned around. "That was easy."

Dandy staggered a little, like the dictionary had knocked him silly. "Yeah, for you."

"Think I scared him off?" Malcolm said.

Dandy stopped swaying and rubbed his head. "I hope so. But maybe I should go get my helmet just to be sure."

They waited a few more seconds, just in case.

"Wow," Dandy said. "I don't know why that old guy was so mad. I got the answers right."

No sooner were the words out of his mouth when—*bleep-bleep-bleep.*

The ghost popped up behind Dandy and grabbed him in a ghostly choke hold. "Malcolm!" Dandy cried.

"You got the answer wrong!" the ghost said, holding Dandy tight. He lifted him like a human shield.

Malcolm raised the zapper, but if it sprayed now, it would hit Dandy. "Hang in there," he told his friend.

"H-E-L-P!" Dandy spelled out. "M-A-L-C-O-L-M!" Dandy's eyes grew wide as he tried to clutch his throat. "H-E-L-P!"

The ghost laughed.

Malcolm moved toward them, but the ghost backed up, keeping Dandy close.

"H-E-L-P!" Dandy hollered again.

"Why are you spelling everything?" Malcolm asked.

"C-a-n-n-o-t t-a-l-k."

So this spelling bee specter can do more than just bop someone with a dictionary, Malcolm thought. "What are you doing to him?"

The ghost flashed his oversize teeth. "Just making him a better speller."

"He's already a good speller," Malcolm said. "Who are you anyway?"

"The name's Bernie. Bernie Baxter."

With his bow tie he definitely looked like a Bernie.

"Why are you haunting the spelling bee?" Malcolm asked.

Bernie snarled. "You call that a spelling bee? I hosted over 200 in my day. They were symphonies compared to this dog and pony show. Thankfully, my bees cleared out the bee." The ghost squeezed Dandy tighter.

"So you sent in that swarm!" Malcolm exclaimed.

The ghost's mouth curled into a creepy grin. "Of course. I love a good play on words."

"You need to let Dandy go," Malcolm said. "He got your stupid quiz right. Let him go."

"P-l-e-a-s-e," Dandy begged.

"He didn't get it right," the ghost insisted. "For one thing, you don't spell *doughnut* d-o-n-u-t."

"You can nowadays," Malcolm said. "It's a new spelling."

"Oh yeah?" Baxter said. "Well you don't spell *opossum* with the *o*."

Malcolm shook his head. "You do if it's a possum in Australia. Those are a different species than the ones we have here. I did a report on them."

The ghost's narrow face sagged. "Well what about catsup?"

"What about it?" Malcolm asked. "Both spellings are correct." He lowered his zapper and tilted his head. "Is that why you're haunting the spelling bee? You don't like how people spell things these days?"

Baxter nodded, looking a little sad.

"Language has always changed over time," Malcolm explained. "If it didn't, we'd all still talk like Shakespeare."

"Y-e-a-h," Dandy croaked.

"So grow up and get over it," Malcolm said. "That's just how language is."

The ghost glanced at the whiteboard, then back at Malcolm. "I guess you're right."

"I know I am."

"If you put down that zapper, I'll put down your friend."

Malcolm nodded. "Deal." He set down the zapper.

Baxter dropped Dandy flat on his rear.

"Ouch!" Dandy cried.

At least he didn't spell it, Malcolm thought. "Now leave us alone so my friend can win the spelling bee."

"All right." He looked down at Dandy. "G-o-o-d l-u-c-k."

Dandy looked up. "T-h-a-n-k-s."

Chapter 11
Final Round

When he got home that afternoon, Malcolm slowly opened the front door. He didn't want to conk his head on Grandma Eunice's exercise machine again. But the living room was back to normal.

Malcolm wandered into the kitchen. His mom stood at the stove boiling hot dogs. Real hot dogs, without kale!

Grandma Eunice sat pouting.

Uh-oh, Malcolm thought. *This can't be good.* He shuffled over. "What's up?"

His mom opened the refrigerator, pulled out the mustard and relish, then slammed the door shut.

"Grandma?" he said, realizing his mom was too upset to talk.

Grandma Eunice scowled. He didn't think it was possible, but the wrinkles on her forehead grew deeper. "It's not fair," she mumbled under her breath.

"What's not fair?" he asked.

Grandma Eunice clenched her fists, her nostrils flaring. "I got kicked out of Super Savers."

Malcolm looked at his mom. She was chopping an onion into teeny bits. "You were lucky you didn't get arrested," she said.

"What?!" Malcolm whipped his head back to Grandma Eunice.

She clacked her dentures. "It wasn't my fault. I was at ShopMart, about to buy the last pack of TidyWipe toilet paper. Just fifty cents with my Super Savers coupon. That's when Trudy showed up. She claimed she saw it first and ripped it from my hands."

"What did you do?" Malcolm asked.

"What do you think I did?" she answered. "I wasn't going to let that old fusspot get my toilet paper. I snatched it back."

Malcolm tilted his head. "And?"

"And she wouldn't let go."

"So what happened?"

Grandma Eunice waggled her eyebrows. "I let go. Trudy tumbled back, knocking over a rack of colas. Some opened, spewing out all over the window. A bunch of others rolled down the aisles, tripping customers. I wheeled to the cash register as fast as I

could, but I didn't know that the toilet paper had come loose and stuck to the shampoo shelf. And TidyWipe is some tough toilet paper."

Tough toilet paper? *Ouch,* Malcolm thought. *No wonder it was on sale.*

"I left a trail of toilet paper that knocked down the shampoo, making the floor even more slippery. One customer fell so hard I don't think he'll be sitting for a week."

"Grandma, that's terrible."

She grinned. "But the good news is, Trudy got kicked out too."

Malcolm inhaled the aroma of hot dogs. *That's not the only good news,* he thought.

The following Saturday morning, the community center was packed. It was the

final round of the spelling bee. And so far, not a ghostly creature was to be found.

Mr. McDonaldson sat in his bee master chair, his hair slicked back. "Contestant number one," he said.

Contestant number one, a boy who looked like he was eating the microphone every time he spelled a word, nodded.

"Your word is *detector*," Mr. McDonaldson said.

The boy planted his lips on the microphone. "Detector. D-e-t-e-c-t-e-r. Detector."

Buzzzzzzz.

The boy pulled back, his eyes round with disbelief.

"Sorry," Mr. McDonaldson said. He then turned to Dandy, the only contestant left. "If you can spell this word correctly, you

will be this year's champion. The word is
detector."

Dandy's grin was so big, it shone brighter
than his future trophy.

Questions for You

From Ghost Detectors
Malcolm and Dandy

Dandy: I was so nervous for the spelling bee. I didn't want to let my family down! Have you ever felt this way? What happened?

Dandy: Malcolm is my best friend. He even came to the spelling bee to cheer me on! Do you have a best friend? What do you do to support him or her?

Malcolm: I had a feeling a ghost was behind all those weird things that happened at the spelling bee. Have you ever had a strong feeling about something? Were you right?

Malcolm: I taught the spelling bee specter a few things about spelling so he'd stop haunting the contest. What would you have done if you were in my place?